BRANDON STEVENSON

Eddie Versus
the Shadow Shifters
in the Battle for Christmas

MONKEY BRAIN FACTORY, INC.

monkeybrainfactory.com

ISBN 978-0-692-93725-9

Printed in the United States of America

Contents

I   Where Are You, Christmas?   1

II   Spy Games and Shifty Characters   15

III   The North Pole and the ER   23

IV   The World of Shadows   31

V   From the North Pole to Brookville   35

VI   I Have a Plan   47

VII   Two More Days   53

VIII   The Race   61

IX   Christmas Trees and Christmas Cheer   67

X   The Last Day   79

XI   The Shadow Shifters Are Coming   89

XII   Light from Darkness   95

XIII   Christmas Morning   105

The Adventures of Eddie Continue   119

Sneak Peak of *Eddie Versus the Creature in the Woods: A Mission to Save Summer Camp*   121

I

WHERE ARE YOU, CHRISTMAS?

As they drove up the hill into Brookville, the town that would be their new home, snow continued to fall, creating a white blanket as far as Eddie could see. He was writing on a wrinkly piece of paper that was pressed against the book in his lap. Reaching the top of the hill presented a different view and captured his attention. "We're here, aren't we?"

His father chuckled. They had been driving for hours while Eddie quizzed his parents about their third move in as many years. His questions included how long they would live here, what the house and town were like, and whether Dad's work would make them move again next year. It wasn't long ago that Eddie had stopped asking questions and allowed his parents to talk quietly in the front seat while he focused on his letter to Santa. Now, though, they knew that there was no stopping him until they arrived at their new home. Sometimes it was exhausting, but Eddie was always alert and aware. Alan could see his son in the rearview mirror scribbling away while occasionally looking up and taking in the sights of their new town just ahead.

Brookville's town square included a row of shops, a frozen lake currently occupied by a small group of ice-skaters, some large trees that Eddie imagined covered in Christmas lights at night, and a cobblestone bridge that crossed the now frozen stream that fed the lake. Eddie quickly began questioning his parents about each house that he saw, hoping to spot his new home. "Is that it?" Eddie asked as they approached the first house in the neighborhood.

"No, not that one," his mother replied, smiling and looking back at Eddie, who was breathing heavily against the window while fidgeting with his captain's hat.

"What about that one?" Eddie continued, hoping that each house he spotted would be theirs.

"Nope, not that one, Eddie."

Eddie rested his head against the window and released a long sigh. He was becoming anxious; he had hoped that the ride would have been over already so he could unpack and begin exploring his new neighborhood before the sun set and his mother wouldn't let him leave the house. Though it had been less than thirty seconds since he asked about the previous home, he couldn't contain himself. "Mom … are we close?"

There was a pause of only a couple of seconds before he received a response, but to Eddie those seconds felt like a lifetime. Finally she pointed ahead and responded, "Yes, that's the one!"

Eddie wiped the foggy window so he could see more clearly. As the new home came into view, his mouth dropped open in amazement. He pressed his face to the window, and his captain's hat fell back onto the seat. The house looked incredible, and that window had to be his. He knew it would be. The window at the top of the circular tower that highlighted the second floor of his new home was perfect! The window looked right toward his new town and would be his companion, providing a great view of the town square as he began to explore. Eddie noticed that he couldn't see inside as they approached the house—the high window provided only a reflection. That would be very useful, as Eddie could take advantage of the privacy it provided. He could use his high perch to keep an eye out for bad guys, secret agents, and monsters until he made new friends who could be part of his spy team.

Sophie, Eddie's mom, knew that her own interests had rubbed off on Eddie. She had always wanted to pursue a writing career. After Eddie was born, she began focusing on her dream of balancing her writing with the challenges of being a stay-at-home mom. Over the years, she had become a fairly well-known novelist thanks to the success of her detective series, which followed a seasoned officer through his toughest cases in gritty Los Angeles.

Eddie showed interest in what his mom was working on from an early age. She began to adapt fun short stories based on the novels' characters for him to read. It wasn't long before Eddie began asking for detective equipment and spy gear so he could investigate anything he found suspicious.

Sophie thought about how quickly Eddie's reading capabilities had advanced and how inspired he was after every story he digested as she turned around to look at him. "Are you ready to see your new room?" He nodded his head and Sophie smiled as they pulled into the driveway.

The house was already warm, and the movers were finishing packing the last few boxes into the living room as they arrived. Eddie asked his parents if his room was

4

upstairs. After being told to run upstairs and check, he knew that his guess was correct.

The tower would be his!

He was right about another thing, too. His view was perfect—he could see the entire town square. As excited as he was about his new room, he knew he had work to do. His parents told him that he had to unpack before he could explore the neighborhood, but he only had so much time before sunset. If he didn't finish quickly, he would have to wait until the next day. As he knocked the other boxes over that were stacked on top of his gear, he noticed that the movers had followed the instructions that were written on the side of the first box. The bold black writing clearly read, "Eddie's Spy Equipment—Do **NOT** Open!!!" The second box had a drawing of a Christmas tree on the side that Eddie had made with crayons while waiting for the movers to pack everything up at their old house.

It took nearly two hours, but he had put away all of his clothes, organized his closet, made his bed, and put up his personal Christmas tree in his room. That should be enough to allow him to go outside for the evening.

The binoculars were now around his neck, hanging comfortably by the strap Eddie had made from an old shoelace. He had placed the rest of his equipment underneath the bed for safekeeping while he went to explore his new neighborhood. Meanwhile, the miniature Christmas tree was glowing brightly on his dresser near the window. Eddie smiled from the doorway as he looked at the multicolored lights that illuminated the walls and ceiling of his new bedroom. He felt better about the move already.

Just before running downstairs, Eddie stopped at his doorway and surveyed his bedroom one last time. The scraps of cardboard on the floor were evidence of the hard work that Eddie had put in to open the boxes as quickly as possible. What was once a box was now pieces of shredded cardboard all over the floor. It would have to be cleaned up to avoid further inspection by his parents. Luckily, it only took a minute to scoop it all up and deposit the scraps out of sight in the back of his closet.

As he came down the stairs and entered the kitchen, he found his mother unpacking dishes and his father emptying several brown bags full of groceries into the refrigerator.

"Mom, Dad, can we go get a Christmas tree tomorrow? Christmas is only a few days away."

After a brief smile, Eddie's father nodded his head in agreement. "As soon as we finish unpacking, we'll get the best tree we can find!" With a quick jump and a cheer, Eddie moved toward the front door.

"Where are you running off to, Eddie?" his mom asked as she placed dishes into the cabinets.

"I just want to look around before it gets dark, Mom."

As she turned around, Eddie already knew what she was about to say. He was prepared to beg, but he didn't have to.

His father interrupted. "Honey, let's give him an hour to play."

She looked at Alan uneasily without responding.

"We could use the time to unpack, and he's been in the car all day long. I'm sure a little running around outside would be good. Right, Eddie?" He looked over and winked at Eddie, who smiled and nodded.

Finally his mother asked, "Did you finish unpacking your room?" Eddie nodded. "Okay, you can go play for one hour, Eddie, but don't go wandering in the forest or past the lake. This is a new area, so be careful. We'll have to explore together, okay?"

Eddie nodded, anxious for his mom to allow him to leave.

"Alright, set your watch and be back on time."

One quick push of a button on his multifunction

watch with audio recorder, and off he went.

"And wear your coat," he heard his mother shout as he ran toward the door.

Eddie had left it on the floor near the entryway. He scooped it up and pulled it over his head as he ran out the door.

Quickly reaching the bottom of the hill, Eddie made his way to the Brookville town square. The small shops were great, each one with a little wooden sign above the door, and the streets were made of stone. As he approached the square, Eddie noticed that the most centrally located area included a clearing with a large fountain, benches, and several levels of what would likely be landscaped plants in summer. However, since it was three days before Christmas, none of this was visible under the blanket of beautiful white snow. Eddie suddenly had a thought ...

Today was December twenty-second. Did Brookville not have a town Christmas tree?

He looked around at every detail he could see within the town square. He looked at each shop, house, window, rooftop, stoop, and front door. Eddie spent several minutes examining his surroundings. Why weren't there any Christmas trees? Why weren't there any Christmas lights, wreaths, or other decorations? The sidewalk in front of the toy store was empty, too.

Eddie remembered the crowds of kids who would gather in front of the toy store in his old town, waiting for the next fancy display to be revealed. He remembered how impatient he had been while waiting among the crowd to see the newest window displays, which were updated daily as Christmas approached. He remembered daydreaming about the adventures that each toy would provide if Santa Claus brought it to him on Christmas Day. Each new display in the window made the approaching decision even more difficult. Eddie always knew that he had to choose wisely; not every toy would arrive under his Christmas tree, even if he had been nice all year long.

Brookville seemed different. No, it was *definitely* different. The only thing occupying the space in front of this toy store and the amazing display in the window— which Eddie had already decided deserved his attention—was a mound of snow. While making his way over to the toy store, Eddie stopped in the middle of the town square. He stopped right where there should have been a huge Christmas tree with colorful lights and beautiful decorations contributed by everyone in town. It was easy for Eddie to imagine a tree right here. He loved Christmas, and every town he had lived in did, too—that is, every town other than this one.

Now that he was standing in front of the window display, it was even more impressive. A bicycle was suspended in midair, its front wheel aimed downward as if about to land a jump. Beneath the suspended bicycle was a lake with a crocodile looking up, its mouth open with all of its sharp teeth showing. Eddie imagined himself as a daredevil completing this stunt as the neighborhood kids cheered him on. He smiled at the thought and considered asking Santa for a new bike for Christmas. Maybe he would, but there were other things on his list.

It was getting late and would be dark soon. Eddie didn't have much time; he knew he needed to be home within the hour to avoid getting in trouble. He decided to step out of the cold and into the toy store, just for a quick visit. As he passed through the entryway into the main part of the store, he noticed an old man with glasses sitting behind the counter. The man hadn't noticed that anyone had entered the store. His head was propped on his hands, and he was looking in the direction of a small television. Eddie couldn't tell if the man was watching TV or sleeping, so he approached quietly and announced his presence softly. "Excuse me, sir."

The man jumped, slightly startled.

"Oh yes, I didn't see you come in … what can I do for you, son?" The man spoke softly and seemed friendly.

"I'm Eddie. I just moved here today."

The man adjusted his glasses and looked at Eddie. "Oh yes, the house just up the hill. Do you need help with anything? Are there any toys that you like?"

After a moment of silence, the man began to speak again, fumbling over his words as he did. "Ohhh, where are my mann … I completely for … I should have introduced myself. I'm Frank!"

Eddie smiled and thought for a moment before looking back toward the entrance.

"Well, I just walked in, but the bicycle in the window is great, and the display is one of the best I've ever seen!"

Frank chuckled as he glanced toward the display. He thanked Eddie for noticing and invited him to browse the store.

"I don't have much time before I have to be back home. But I may ask for that bicycle for Christmas. Can you tell me why there are no Christmas decorations on your store? Or in Brookville at all? Christmas is almost here!"

Frank seemed puzzled.

"Christmas—yes, that's soon. Just around the corner, you say?"

Eddie's jaw nearly hit the floor. This man works in a toy store, and he doesn't know that Christmas is only a few days away?

"Christmas is less than a week away. It's the biggest time of the year for toys. Why don't you have Christmas songs and Christmas offers and a Christmas tree?" Eddie became very excited, throwing his arms in the air as he finished the sentence, but Frank didn't seem bothered by this at all. He just scratched his head as if he was really giving Eddie's question some thought.

"Well, to be honest with you, I don't know. I guess we just don't really get too involved with Christmas around here ..." Frank trailed off.

"You mean no one celebrates Christmas? Why not?!"

Eddie had gone from wandering around in front of the counter to leaning over it, nearly nose to nose with Frank. He was very confused by the vague explanation and needed to know more, but Frank didn't seem to have an answer. It was as if Christmas was a distant childhood memory that he couldn't quite recall.

Without another word between them, Eddie walked back out into the snow, feeling even more confused, while Frank stood still scratching his head, seemingly lost in his own cloudy memories. It was getting even colder outside. Eddie didn't care much about the cold, though. He wondered why everyone was too busy to notice or care about Christmas. And why had Frank become so confused?

This is the biggest, most exciting holiday of the year, Eddie thought. *Everyone loves Christmas.*

That's when it hit him—something had gone wrong. Everything seemed perfect, yet he had never seen a town in his ten and a half years that didn't have a Christmas tree on display.

Yes, he determined, *something was definitely wrong here.*

II

SPY GAMES AND SHIFTY CHARACTERS

Having walked around sulking for several minutes, Eddie decided that he must take matters into his own hands. Using his binoculars, he was already investigating potential culprits, hoping to spot a shifty character from afar. First, he spotted a middle-aged couple walking arm in arm nearby. Everything about them seemed pretty normal. Eddie quickly decided that they weren't suspects and moved on. Having made his way down the slight incline next to the stream that in springtime would feed the lake, he found cover behind some small bushes. He was on the edge of the now frozen stream and had a pretty nice vantage point. It would be necessary to reposition himself if he wanted a view of the entire town, though. He decided that he would explore a significant area from this location, which conveniently allowed him to remain fully camouflaged. This was an absolute necessity to effectively spy on the strangers who populated this unfamiliar town.

Nearly twenty minutes had passed, and Eddie had no suspects. The small group he observed on the frozen lake were merely ice-skating with seemingly no other motive. The consequence of the weather limited the potential suspects, as it seemed much of the town had opted to remain indoors and avoid the frozen wind that occasionally picked up and carried the powdery snow with it. Only nine potential suspects had passed. Five of them were ice-skating, two walked through the town square holding each other tight in an effort to stay warm, and the last two were other kids who were chasing each other while launching fierce snowball attacks as often as possible. Eddie watched them from his hidden location for a minute, tracking them as they ran. They looked to be his age and candidates for new friends.

Suddenly Eddie noticed a strange movement from the bushes across the pond. It was closer to Eddie than the snowball battle. Tracking back slightly and refocusing his binoculars, he spotted the movement in the bush again. Just as he did, the small bush flipped over as if it had fallen out of the ground. Eddie was now completely frozen in nervous excitement; perhaps it was due to lying in the snow for twenty minutes as well, but he knew he had found something important as a small head popped out of the hole in the ground where the bush had just been.

Following a quick look around, the character hopped out of the hole and placed the bush back in place, concealing his hidden entrance to Brookville. Eddie continued to watch through his binoculars while recording as much as he could in his head. The man looked to be no taller than Eddie. He was wearing a tactical-looking outfit with pockets and pouches all over his pants and vest. It was also camouflage—the kind Eddie had seen in movies that spies or soldiers wear in the snow. Wearing a small backpack that looked to be custom-made for a man of his size, he quickly made his way to a building and began to scale one of the pipes that ran vertically toward the roof. His movement was quick, intentional, and precise.

This was definitely the shifty fellow Eddie had been looking for. He had a mission; that was obvious by the way he moved. Eddie didn't want to lose him, but as the man disappeared over the peak of the roof, it was obvious that Eddie would not be able to catch him. He was agile and, unfortunately, a much better climber than Eddie.

Since Eddie had lost him, it was obviously best to investigate the method he had used to enter the town. Making his way across the pond would be faster than going around, but since Eddie didn't have ice skates, the frozen lake would probably be too slippery to cross.

Moments later, Eddie was running at full speed toward the edge of the frozen lake. Slippery or not, he knew this would be the quickest way to accomplish his mission. The last step was more of a hop, which landed him in a balanced surfer's stance. The momentum carried him forward, and he maintained his balance as he glided across the ice. Near the middle of the lake, his momentum ran out and he slowed to a stop. The ice-skaters were on the other side of the lake but still took notice. Eddie could hear them cheering as he tried to run across the part of the lake that still lay in front of him. The attention was something that he didn't want right now. He wanted privacy, which would allow him to investigate the secret entrance that this Christmas-stealing culprit had used to sneak into town. Eddie's investigation could help him determine whom the man worked for and what they were up to.

Now, only a few seconds after the groups of ice-skaters cheered, laughter began to erupt. A quick glance their way revealed one of them lying on the ice following what must have been quite the comedic crash.

Now that the attention was no longer on Eddie, he quickly hopped behind the row of bushes upon reaching the edge of the lake. The cover allowed him a moment to think about his next move. Was he going to just open the bush? Could he? If he did just open it, was he going to simply look? What would he find down there? The picture of a dark underground world full of monsters popped into Eddie's head, but he quickly pushed it aside. He had a mission and couldn't get scared now. While crawling closer to the bush, he couldn't tell whether it was the run across the lake or the fear of the unknown that was causing his heart to pound and his breath to be quick and heavy.

It was only a few feet away now, and Eddie's heartbeat was audible. The rapid and constant **thump-thump, thump-thump** was all he could hear. He took a look around; the kids who were throwing snowballs were long gone, while the kids who were ice-skating were still laughing and joking. Eddie could barely hear them, though. His heartbeat had taken over and was drowning out everything else. **Do it now**, Eddie thought to himself as he sat right in front of the bush, *before you lose your nerve.* But would he just pull on the bush? He didn't know what to do, and he was now crippled by fear and unable to move.

How much time had passed? Eddie figured it could have only been a minute ago at most that he closed his eyes and banished the thought of monsters and an underground city that mirrored his own. The sound of his heartbeat was gone now, and as he looked around he noticed that he was still alone. It was time. He reached around the base of the bush, trying to find an edge that he could lift, but there was nothing. He pulled on the bush itself, but it didn't budge. He moved closer, placing his face right next to the base of the bush, looking for a clue about how to unearth it. This was definitely the right one, but he figured it must be locked to protect the Christmas bandits.

He looked again at the base of the bush. The lines in the wood seemed to come together in one area to form a circle. As Eddie moved closer, he noticed what looked like tiny letters in the middle of the circle. Although he was only inches away, he still had to squint. It looked as though the letters said "ER." A soft touch of these letters, and the entire area where the bush was planted made a popping sound. Suddenly an edge was revealed.

Before he could even pull on it, a hatch opened before Eddie's eyes.

Darkness.

He peered in, but he couldn't see anything—it was completely black. Leaning a bit closer didn't seem to help; his face was nearly even with the hole in the ground, and it looked as if nothing existed, not even dirt. As he reached his hand in to feel for the edges of the hole, an invisible force took Eddie by surprise and pulled him into the darkness.

III

THE NORTH POLE AND THE ER

He was falling. Falling through the darkness into what seemed to be endless nothingness. It was almost as if time was standing still for Eddie. He could feel himself falling. Thoughts were flying through his head. Where was he falling to? Why didn't he just go home and tell his parents what he saw? What was he going to do? As questions bounced through his head, everything around him began to light up. The light was so bright that, even though it was the opposite of the earlier darkness, he still couldn't see anything.

Eddie was scared.

In one instant, the world around Eddie morphed into flashes of brilliant color. They weren't just colors, though—they felt inviting and comforting. As Eddie's eyes were finally able to focus on this mystery world, it looked as though he was traveling through a tube—a giant slide, perhaps—but it was fast, and unlike any slide he had ever been on, this one was pure light. Red, green, gold, and white light. Eddie had no idea where he was going, but he began to feel at ease—happy even. It felt as if he was slowing down when he started to hear the faint sound of bells and smell a familiar aroma. It smelled like cookies—chocolate chip and gingerbread for sure. One final flash of brilliant light and he stopped.

The flash had Eddie seeing spots—blinking spots of all colors in front of him. As his eyes focused, he realized that these blinking spots did exist. They were Christmas lights. Eddie looked down and noticed that he had landed on a golden platform. It was a gentle landing, and he wasn't hurt at all. He hopped down from the platform and took a few steps forward before spotting a doorway. The room, which was small and circular, contained nothing but the shining golden platform, some Christmas decorations, and the darkened doorway that he was now approaching.

Once again, Eddie found himself slightly afraid, but he wasn't sure why. This place not only looked like every Christmas tale he could remember, but it made him feel happy. He figured the thing that was bothering him was that he didn't know where this place was. He could be anywhere. Standing before the dim doorway wasn't going to solve anything, so he worked up his courage, stepped closer to the door, and read the inscription aloud: "The North Pole – Elf Rangers." After a moment, Eddie realized what he had just read, and he wanted to scream.

The North Pole!

Had he just traveled to the North Pole? Excitement had now overtaken any fear that still existed. He opened the door.

The Toy Factory filled with happy elves sliding down poles, swinging from Christmas-colored ropes, assembling toys, and happily singing popular Christmas songs in sync; this is what Eddie knew he would find on the other side of the door. Those things existed in every Christmas story he had ever read and every Christmas movie he had ever seen. Once he was there, he would be taken to the Head Elf, who would explain to Eddie that he shouldn't be there, but he would give Eddie a tour and they would talk. Finally, Eddie would wake up in his bed, knowing that he hadn't just awakened from a dream. There would be a small reminder from his elf friends that would assure him that he **had** in fact been to the North Pole. Eddie knew that all of this would happen. It was like a dream come true.

Eddie was wrong.

Instead, the room had a giant digital map with markings on it that looked more like a war game than Santa's present-delivery strategy. There were elves seated in rows, looking at the map. They were all dressed like the small man Eddie observed as he climbed out of what now seemed like a portal that connected Eddie's town to the North Pole.

There was one elf who was obviously in charge, lecturing to the other elves as information popped onto the screen. Eddie moved slowly, crouching behind a pillar near the door. Unfortunately, all the thoughts of happy Christmas tales, the Toy Factory, and candy were nonexistent in the world that Eddie found himself in.

Perhaps this wasn't really the North Pole, he thought. The next five minutes felt a lot like the introduction to a terrifying horror film.

The man who was in charge continued to speak.

Shadow Shifters!

They looked horrible and, by the description, they sounded even scarier. Existing in darkness and creeping along the surfaces of any location they desired within shadows, they traveled undetected.

Shadow Shifters only showed life when they approached or attacked, remaining hidden until they were ready to pounce.

Even worse, they were taking over Eddie's new town and attempting to remove the memory of Christmas altogether. From what Eddie could gather, the Shadow King and his followers were growing stronger due to the lack of Christmas spirit. Every time someone abandoned the holiday spirit and every time a child landed on the naughty list, the Shadow King became more powerful and the darkness became more dangerous.

But what was the answer?

Christmas! Christmas was the answer. The people Eddie was watching were the Elf Rangers. He determined that they were like Santa's private Christmas defenders. Over the years of battling the Shadow Shifters, and probably many other dark forces, they learned that they had to keep the Christmas spirit alive. The entire town needed the spirit of Christmas, though. This, along with good deeds in the name of

Christmas and especially colorful Christmas lights, were powerful defense against the Shadow Shifters. They could not exist within any area illuminated by Christmas lights. The power of the lights would actually destroy them.

Eddie knew exactly what he had to do. He would bring the Christmas spirit to his new town. He would battle the Shadow Shifters using everything he had just learned. He would …

"Who are you, and what exactly are you doing here?"

The voice was gruff, accented, and very direct.

Eddie had been spotted. But by who?!

There was no way for anyone to sneak in behind him unless he had missed another door that allowed entry into the room with the golden platform.

The voice was loud enough to gain the attention of the man who was speaking to the room of Elf Rangers. This, in turn, directed the attention of the entire room to Eddie's location. He could hear whispers and questions among the Elf Rangers who were seated. Slowly and timidly, Eddie turned and looked up, expecting to see a man behind him.

Nothing.

Turning his gaze downward revealed the gruff-sounding man. Though Eddie was only ten and a half and not exactly big for his age, he was still taller than the Elf Ranger who was questioning him. It was the man Eddie first saw entering Brookville from underneath the bush—the first Elf Ranger Eddie ever saw. Now he was being watched by an entire troop of them and was obviously an intruder. He had been a careless spy, and now he had to face the consequences.

Eddie began to speak but stumbled over his words. He took a moment to collect himself and was finally able to get out a short explanation.

"I saw you come through the bush," Eddie gulped.

IV

THE WORLD OF SHADOWS

Thousands of miles away, a dark and silent figure moved stealthily along the cavern floor, appearing and disappearing as the moonlight filtered through the openings overhead. It glided with ease, leaving no footprints or marks to reveal that anyone had traveled this path. The cave itself was a work of art. The openings were evenly placed every couple of feet, allowing just enough moonlight into the hallway to provide slight visibility. The hallway, shaped like a perfect arc, was wide enough to allow several people to walk side by side. It extended from the Den of Shadows, where the dark figure originated, to the upcoming Fire Viewing Room, which was occupied by the Shadow King, or, as his servants called him, the Shadow.

From the large doorway ahead, light escaped the

Fire Viewing Room and danced along the opposing walls. The light revealed shadows that grew large and guaranteed to expose a fierce and opposing figure one moment and disappeared completely the next moment, leaving only a fiery glow to greet the approaching visitor.

As the stealthy figure approached the large doorway, it peeled away from the floor and began gaining mass. Before entering the room, it had morphed from a dark, flat creature into a shape that somewhat resembled a man. It had a head, shoulders, and arms, but did not have skin, hair, eyes, a tongue, or a heart.

It was imposing, standing over six feet tall, though its shape was never constant. Upon entering the room, it scattered but quickly reappeared on the opposite side of the room and again on the walls surrounding the fire that flickered in the middle of the room. Finally it appeared behind the dark figure that had been waiting impatiently in the room. The waiting creature looked similar, though it was much larger and seemingly more powerful.

The approaching figure quickly knelt, validating his role as a servant, and finally made a sound.

"My Lord …" hissed a voice that was both hideous and deceptive. The sound traveled through the room as if it had been carried by the wind and not spoken by the figure at all.

The Shadow King didn't turn to greet his servant. Instead, he lifted from the ground with ease and transformed in midair while hurtling his body much closer to the servant, who was still kneeling.

"What news do you bring, Vesh?" he boomed as he came within inches of Vesh's face.

Shrinking backward, Vesh's voice lifted higher than before. "It was a boy. He went into the Brookville transport only minutes ago."

"What? Christmas doesn't exist in Brookville anymore. Not a single Christmas tree has been placed in a home, not a single present has been purchased. Why would anyone enter the transport, and HOW does he know about it?"

The Shadow grew larger as his voice grew deeper, filling with rage.

He lifted from the floor again and catapulted himself toward the wall like a missile, darting along the wall and quickly traveling around and around the circular room. The wind caused the fire to shift as the Shadow growled loudly. The center of the fire died down, revealing the hot coals beneath. He quickly bounced from the wall back to the center of the room, hovering over the coals as dark, glowing pits formed where eyes would be. Vesh remained silent while the Shadow took a moment to peer at the coals.

The coals flickered as a dark, silhouetted scene became visible from within. It revealed an event that had just taken place in Brookville. Eddie walked into the toy store and began to ask the shop owner about Christmas …

V

FROM THE NORTH POLE TO BROOKVILLE

Eddie and Theodore—the Elf Ranger Eddie first spotted entering Brookville from under the bush—stood next to the golden platform. Eddie had learned a lot while spying on the Elf Rangers at the North Pole—a lot that he shouldn't know, but it would help him combat the Shadow Shifters and protect his new home. It didn't matter that Theodore, along with the other Elf Rangers, told him that it was too dangerous and that they wouldn't allow him to join them. They couldn't stop him from using his knowledge to prepare for the Shadow Shifters, and they couldn't stop him from spreading Christmas cheer all around Brookville.

Just before stepping onto the golden platform for the journey back to Brookville, Theodore stopped.

"You know, you're a brave kid."

Eddie smiled as Theodore continued.

"They might be aware of you. Just keep some Christmas lights in your room, eh?"

A smaller and friendlier-looking elf walked in and handed a rope of lights to Theodore, telling him that they had just finished making the lights in the workshop.

The workshop!

"Theodore, can I see the workshop before we go? I really, really, really want to. Can we take a tour?"

Having been distracted by the news of the Shadow Shifters, Eddie had completely forgotten about the toy shop tour he had envisioned—the tour that every kid who goes to the North Pole gets in every Christmas story. Theodore paused and seemed to consider it, finally looking toward Eddie, slightly disappointed.

"I like you, kid, but I just can't do it. We will already have our hands full explaining to the Claus how you even made it here."

"I'll help explain. I can tell him how I snuck in and explain that I can help."

"No can do, but I'll stop and check in on you. Now come on, let's get on the move."

Theodore hopped onto the platform with ease, even though it hovered above the floor at nearly the height of his waist. Eddie kicked at the ground and mumbled a bit as he prepared to climb onto the golden platform. Theodore reached his hand to assist and pulled Eddie up with ease and strength that surprised Eddie.

"Now, I'm not sure how the trip here was for you—none of us have ever traveled back without calling the platform to carry us—but I'm sure this will be a bit different."

"Different how?"

Theodore smiled.

It was the first time Eddie had seen him smile. The tough scowl quickly returned to Theodore's face, but it was too late. He worked hard to maintain his tough guy look, but his smile revealed everything to Eddie. *He's a good guy, and he's not as tough as he pretends to be.*

Suddenly Eddie's thoughts were interrupted by a sudden jolt that made his brain hurt, followed by flashes of light. The next thing he knew, Theodore was helping him up. He was dizzy and confused.

They were back already? Theodore was already working away. He activated a control panel on the pitch-black wall, which caused multiple screens to illuminate, showing a real-time view of the area surrounding the bush that would allow them to reenter Brookville.

"The platform is fast. It's a bit overwhelming the first time, but you get used to it."

Theodore explained this to Eddie while scanning the surrounding area. Once he was sure that the area was clear, he pushed a sequence of buttons that caused the ceiling to pop open as the golden platform slowly began to rise. Theodore took another quick look through the crack in the hatch above and finally pushed it open. Both Eddie and Theodore climbed out. The sun had already begun to set, and there was just a bit of light left in the sky. It was past time for Eddie to be home. He was going to be in trouble. A quick look at his watch revealed that he was more than thirty minutes late.

Strange, Eddie thought, *the alarm on his watch didn't function while at the North Pole.* It didn't matter. He couldn't tell his parents where he had been, and he would definitely be in trouble.

"It's almost dark. Hurry home, Eddie. Put those lights in your room, too. Surely the Shadow King is watching you by now. He may be aware of your interactions with the Elf Rangers. You'll want to be careful, as Christmas is near and he'll be aggressive. Don't try to be a hero, Eddie. The Elf Rangers will take care of Brookville, and Christmas will be just as you've always known it."

Though Eddie had no intention of hiding in his room while the Elf Rangers did all the work, he nodded in agreement.

"Thanks, Theodore."

He turned to leave, and while it was barely noticeable, a tiny smile crept onto Theodore's face as he watched the brave boy walk away.

"Hey Theodore …" Eddie said as he turned back around.

"Yeah, kid?"

"Why do the Shadow Shifters want Brookville?"

Theodore paused and furled his brow.

"It's complicated. See, the Shadow King used to be an Elf Ranger before he turned to darkness."

Eddie's eyes widened.

"His name was Seth back then. He held my position as Commander of the Rangers and trained me when I graduated from the Ranger Program. Seth mentored me and became one of my closest friends as I moved up in the ranks to second in command and worked alongside him. Over the years, though, he started to change. He was seeking power and control. Eventually, Seth became aggressive. He attempted to sabotage Santa and told all of us that he should be in charge of Christmas.

"Santa removed him from the Ranger Program and everything changed. Seth left the North Pole, and I was promoted to Commander. I tried to reach out to him soon after, but he didn't respond. The next time I saw him, he was different. His eyes were dark, like coal, and he was angry. Evil eventually overtook him, and he became the Shadow."

Theodore continued, "He's been banished from the North Pole, and the portal is full of powerful lights that he would not survive due to the evil within him. It's believed, however, that if he can take control of Brookville, he can also take the portal on Christmas Day, turn it to darkness, and return to the North Pole to seek his revenge."

Eddie gulped and began to search his thoughts, but before he could say anything, Theodore added, "I'm sorry, kid. This is heavy stuff, but you've already seen a lot. I think you deserve to know the truth about what's happening in Brookville."

"Is there anyone left in Brookville who remembers Christmas?"

Theodore nodded. "There are only a few others. Make sure to get some lights and decorations up. You'll want the protection, and you may very well be Brookville's last hope."

After a slight nod, Eddie asked, "Do you miss your friend, Theodore?"

Theodore cracked a slight smile again, but this one was a sad smile—one that showed a true moment of emotion that Theodore rarely allowed himself.

"Yes, I do." Those were the only words he could muster.

Eddie paused and looked at his feet, shifting nervously. "Do you promise that I'll see you again?"

"Yeah, I promise. And call me Ted."

Eddie smiled, turned, and took off running toward his house. Ted continued to watch him until Eddie was out of sight and then hopped back into the transport and disappeared from Brookville without anyone else seeing him.

The Shadow King, however, had seen everything, and Ted was right. His newfound friend was in danger. Other than Santa and the Elf Rangers, Eddie was the next-largest obstacle preventing the Shadow Shifters from taking Christmas from Brookville permanently. Two hours ago, the Shadow Shifters had no knowledge of his existence, but now they were watching Eddie closely as he ran toward his house. They didn't just watch him from the comfort of the Fire Viewing Room, either …

As Eddie ran home, he looked up. He could see the moon hanging overhead, preparing to assume control of the sky for the night, while the sun was quickly disappearing behind the distant hills.

Darkness was only minutes away, and the streetlamps had just flickered to life, causing hundreds of shadows to reveal themselves. Eddie was approaching his front yard and could see lights shining through the windows of his new home. However, a movement from a nearby tree just ahead caused Eddie to stop in his tracks. The branches swayed and rustled in the wind while Eddie stood frozen, looking cautiously at the lone shadowed area that remained between him and his home.

As the figure began to grow up from a dark spot in the ground, Eddie cautiously took a step back. He looked around and realized there was nowhere to run.

The figure now resembled the outline of a full-grown man.

Eddie was trapped.

Suddenly the porch lights came to life and illuminated the yard. In an instant, the figure vanished.

"Eddie, what are you doing down there? Come inside—you're already late!" his father called from the doorway. Eddie's father had come to the rescue, just as he had so many times in the past, but this time he didn't realize the danger that was lurking just outside. Sprinting the entire way, Eddie was through the door and inside the house in no time, bringing snow and ice with him.

After a slight scolding from his parents for being late and making a mess as he ran into the house, he was told to clean up for dinner. Without complaint or hesitation, he apologized for being late and for making a mess and then ran upstairs to his room.

He couldn't tell his parents what had happened. They wouldn't believe him if he did, so he thought it would be best to simply begin preparing for what was ahead. Today was the twenty-second of December. He had two full days ahead to create a plan. This also meant two more nights of darkness and danger.

Getting ready for dinner dropped down a notch on

his list, but Eddie didn't want to get into more trouble by not listening to his parents. Even worse, he didn't want to find out what would happen to him if the Shadow Shifters were to capture him.

He only had a few minutes to prevent both, and he couldn't actually hang the lights properly in such limited time. Instead, Eddie began stretching them out near his window and around his bed. He plugged them in, and the lights immediately came to life.

The walls and ceiling in his room transformed from boring white to a world of twinkling color. Beautiful red, blue, yellow, green, and orange light bounced off of every surface. The colors were brighter, richer, and more powerful than Eddie had ever seen before.

Ted must have given him special lights ... magic lights.

Eddie was finishing stretching out the lights for protection when his mother called him for dinner. As he was leaving his room to wash his hands and face in the bathroom, he turned off the overhead light and stopped for a moment, smiling at what he saw. The Christmas lights were even more impressive now, dotting the windowpane and all the room's surfaces with beautiful, rich colors.

Outside, a car belonging to the family that lived

across the street from Eddie was making its way up the street. In the darkness, the streetlights and high beams from the car caused the lighting to shift while the shadows danced along the ground. From the back seat, Jake thought for a moment that he saw a shadow rise up from the ground like a man forming from nothing. As they pulled into their driveway, he was sure he saw the figure look up at the house across the street. Jake closed his eyes and turned away.

As they got out of the car and walked toward his house, Jake was afraid and stayed close to his parents. He didn't want to look back—he was afraid the figure might still be there. As much as he tried not to, something in Jake made him turn his head and look anyway.

To his relief, he saw no one. He did, however, notice something interesting and different—something he couldn't help but share.

"Mom ... Dad," he called. "Look at the lights the new people put up! Look at them!"

The family of three all stared at the colorful lights dotting the upstairs window for a moment and smiled.

After a moment, Jake blurted out, "Christmas lights!"

His mother suggested that they visit the new family

in the morning and welcome them to the neighborhood. Jake and his father both smiled and agreed.

As they entered their house, the warm feeling they felt while admiring Eddie's lights remained. To an innocent bystander, what had just happened would not raise any alarms or even cause a second glance.

To the Shadow King, however, this simple act was significant and warranted his full attention. One new resident had—in less than a day—infected four people in Brookville with the thought of Christmas. Not only was Eddie interfering with the people of the town and all the hard work the Shadow Shifters had put into destroying the memory of Christmas, but he had also visited the North Pole and made friends with Ted and the Elf Rangers.

He had to be dealt with!

VI

I HAVE A PLAN

It was late and Eddie was supposed to have been in bed asleep long ago, yet he continued to work under the dim light of his table lamp while the wind and snow rattled his bedroom window.

A safe amount of time had passed since his mother had last poked her head into his room to make sure he had settled into the new house on the first night. He was fast asleep, or so she thought. In fact, he was wide awake and was secretly monitoring his parents.

It was only minutes after she left his room that the familiar sound began. The rhythmic rumble that escaped through the crack under the door came from his father's nostrils. He always snored, and Eddie's mother always fell asleep first. This was routine.

It was time to get to work.

Eddie thought back to all the time he had spent with his father in his workshop. The things he had learned always came in handy when he needed to build things. The first item that Eddie sacrificed was one strand of Christmas lights. Next, he grabbed an old pair of snow pants and a jacket.

For this to work, he would have to create a battery pack to power the lights. Time to sacrifice a battery-powered toy.

After nearly two hours of work, he had butchered a battery pack from an old remote control car, connected it to the Christmas lights, and attached them to his pants and jacket. It was time for a test run.

Eddie had created his very own Christmas light suit.

For the first time that night, he unplugged the Christmas lights that were given to him by his new friend, Ted. Fully dressed in his new outfit adorned with multicolored Christmas lights, Eddie walked proudly to the light switch. He looked down at his creation and flipped the switch.

Moonlight entered through the bedroom window and covered a small area of the floor, allowing the rest of the room to remain in darkness. Eddie noticed snowflakes dancing along the outside of the window frame and smiled. In a matter of minutes, it would be the twenty-third of December. Christmas would be here very soon, and everything would be perfect. There would be a lot of work ahead if the plan was going to work, though.

Eddie looked down for a moment to locate the switch on the side of the battery pack that would activate the Christmas lights on his suit. But a moment was all it took for the shadow created by the moonlight streaming through his bedroom window to peel away from the bedroom floor, grow arms, hands, and a face, and reach out to grab Eddie.

The dark hand of the Shadow Shifter wrapped around Eddie's arm just as Eddie's finger touched the switch on his suit. As soon as contact was made, time slowed down and Eddie was stuck for what felt like an eternity, staring into the coal-colored pits that the Shadow Shifter might call eyes.

Eddie could feel his finger on the switch. He could feel the movement in his arm and hand as he attempted to activate the suit. Unfortunately, he couldn't make anything happen, and he didn't know why. Everything began to fade into darkness as Eddie felt his body lift off the ground.

For a moment Eddie thought he was done for, but suddenly an intense flash of colored lights cut through the darkness. Eddie's world became colorful and he felt warm, just as he had at the North Pole.

Just as quickly as the Shadow Shifter had come into Eddie's room, the powerful lights eliminated him. As he burst out of existence before Eddie's eyes, a high-pitched shriek came from the place the Shadow Shifter had just occupied.

The room was now empty. Having looked directly into the bright light, Eddie could hardly see. He was afraid of what had just happened. If he was sure of anything, however, it was that he caught a glimpse of a familiar face during the light show outside of his window.

Ted had come to rescue him!

Still shocked and unsure of the events that had just happened, Eddie quickly flipped the switch on his suit, causing colored light to fill the room. His suit worked, but he had no time to celebrate. He ran to the wall, plugged in the lights he had hung earlier in the day, and flung his window open to look outside. A gust of cold air hit him in the face, and snow fell from the windowsill onto the floor of his room.

He saw nothing. Unsatisfied, he grabbed his binoculars and scanned until he located, next to the lake, the entrance to the portal that had taken him to the North Pole. Just as he located it, a blurry object disappeared down the hatch and the entrance swung shut.

He knew it was Ted.

For the second time that night, Eddie was aware of the danger. This time, there was no mistaking it. He knew this wasn't his imagination. No, the Shadow Shifters were on the hunt, and Eddie would have to protect himself in any way possible. His entire room was lit by two sets of lights now, but he quickly turned off his suit. It would have to be charged and ready for action when he needed it.

VII

TWO MORE DAYS

It was December twenty-third. Christmas was now only two days away. Jake had forgotten about the figure he had seen the previous night as he arrived home, but he had not forgotten the magical lights that illuminated the upstairs window of the new kid who had just moved in across the street.

They were Christmas lights—he remembered that now. After gathering with his parents to marvel at the beautiful glow, he asked why no one else had Christmas lights or a Christmas tree.

"Why aren't we celebrating Christmas?" he quizzed his parents, who seemed just as confused as he was when they realized that Christmas was only days away. After the warm feeling brought on by the Christmas lights, however, it was on all of their minds.

These thoughts and conversations about Christmas that were beginning to resurface in Brookville did not escape the Shadow King. He was in the Fire Viewing Room watching every bit of it and growing angrier by the minute.

It must be stopped!

He would watch every move that Eddie made until Christmas Day. The memory of Christmas was nearly absent from Brookville a day ago, but today the Christmas spirit was growing.

The Shadow King wasn't the only one watching Eddie from afar. Ted and the Elf Rangers were watching Brookville, but more importantly they were continuing to keep an eye on Eddie and working to keep him safe. Just minutes ago, they had been joined by Santa Claus himself. He was given an update on the status of Brookville and how the town's newest resident made his way to the North Pole just a day ago. As Santa knew, Eddie was a bit reckless and very strong-willed, but he was still a good kid. Through the years, Santa had come to know that Eddie would question everything around him, occasionally finding himself in a bit of mischief. Regardless of this, his intentions were always positive, and he was a very interesting boy who never became greedy while crafting his Christmas list.

In fact, his list this year was the most interesting the young boy had created yet.

As Jake continued to stare out the front window, waiting for the new kid to emerge from his house, Jake was unaware that he was actually waiting for the most dangerous kid in Brookville. All eyes were on Eddie, and Jake had no idea what he was getting himself into … yet.

Finally, Eddie emerged from his garage. He was pulling a sled and wearing a large backpack. As he made his way toward the snow-covered street, Jake zipped up his jacket, pulled on his beanie and mittens, and ran out the front door to meet the new kid. Trudging through the snow that had fallen overnight, it only took a few seconds for Eddie to notice that Jake was heading in his direction. He looked up and smiled. It seemed as though it would be much easier to meet new kids in this town than he'd thought.

Jake was a bit shorter than Eddie but looked to be the same age. His face was dotted with freckles, and his hair poked out from underneath his beanie. He was thinner than Eddie as well, yet he looked fairly athletic.

"Hey!" Jake was smiling as he ran up to Eddie. "You just moved here, huh?"

Eddie smiled back as Jake approached. "Yeah, we

got here yesterday. I'm Eddie."

"I'm Jake. Are you going sledding?"

"I don't know," Eddie responded quickly. "What are you going to do?"

Without saying anything, Jake motioned for Eddie to follow him, and they started walking together. As they walked, Jake filled Eddie in on the places to hang out around their neighborhood.

The frozen lake was where kids ice-skated in the winter and swam in the summer. The best hill to go sledding was just beyond the lake along the edge of the forest. There was a clubhouse that Jake and some of the other kids were building in secret using scrap wood and other materials they found.

"You should come when it gets warm and help us finish it!" Jake told Eddie, referring to the clubhouse.

"That sounds awesome. Can we go see it soon?"

Jake said yes but abruptly changed the subject to something that seemed to excite him even more than the clubhouse.

"Are those Christmas lights in your window?!"

Eddie smiled and nodded. The lights amazed Jake, and he began to fire off one question after another about Christmas as if he'd forgotten about it altogether. Eddie knew the reason for Jake's loss of Christmas memories.

The Shadow Shifters.

He couldn't just come out and say it, though—he would have to build up to it.

Eddie was happy. It seemed as though the lights that he'd placed in his window were even more useful than he'd planned. Not only did they look great while protecting him throughout the night, but they also brought Christmas back for Jake.

It had only been about ten minutes since they met, but Eddie could tell that he would like Jake. He was kind and excited about everything. They would be friends, but for now Eddie would have to focus on his plan. There was a battle looming, and he had no time to waste. With that in mind, he began telling Jake more about the Christmas lights.

"Once my parents finish unpacking, we're going to put up more lights—all over the house to light everything up!"

Jake looked at Eddie with growing excitement while Eddie continued to tell him about the Christmas decorations.

"You should come over. We have a ton of lights. I'll give you some so that you can put them on your house, too!"

He knew Jake wouldn't refuse, and he didn't.

Jake gladly accepted and continued to watch Eddie, waiting for the next bit of information as they walked. Eddie paused for a moment and smiled while thinking of Jake and his family putting up Christmas lights. He had just made a friend, brought Christmas back to his friend's family, and reintroduced Christmas to Brookville.

"Does your window face the street?" Eddie asked Jake as he thought about the Shadow Shifters.

Unfortunately, he still couldn't tell Jake about them. They had just met, and Jake probably wouldn't believe Eddie. He might even laugh at him.

Jake nodded his head. "It faces your window. I can see the lights you put up from my room. I asked my parents if I could get some like that to put in my room, too!"

Perfect! *This couldn't be going more smoothly,* Eddie thought as they walked over the bridge that crossed the stream. There were people ice-skating again and some others leaving the town café with steaming drinks to keep them warm. Everyone looked so happy in Brookville; Eddie imagined the town lit up with lights and decorations. He imagined people shopping for presents and kids dropping off their letters to Santa at the post office. Once Ted and the Elf Rangers restored Christmas, this town would be perfect. He just hoped they would get to stay long enough for him to really make friends.

The feeling of sadness only lasted a moment, but Eddie chased it away as quickly as it had come. He didn't like the memory of all the times they had moved in the last three years. He was going to be attending his fourth school once Christmas break was over. His fourth set of friends, and he was still in grade school! That was the past, though—Eddie wouldn't think of it. Jake was his newest friend, and Eddie was on a mission. Everything else would have to wait.

"I'll give you a set of Christmas lights for your room. I have some in my backpack."

Jake cheered. "I'll put them up as soon as I get home, and you'll be able to see them when I plug them in tonight!"

Jake noticed the people walking around with warm drinks. "Do you want to get some hot cocoa?"

Eddie put his hands in his pockets and shrugged. "I can't—I didn't ask my parents for any money before I left home." A quick grin spread across Jake's face.

"No problem—my family owns the café. Let's stop

and get some!"

They ran across the street together with Eddie's sled gliding behind them across the densely packed snow.

VIII

THE RACE

A snowball whizzed past Eddie's face. It was so close that he felt cold water fly off and land on his cheek as it passed by. He was in the final leg of the race and was battling Kevin for first place. The others weren't far behind. Alex was closest, with Jake and Jessica trailing him. Jake had introduced Eddie to everyone just before the race, and it couldn't have been a more varied group. Alex and Jessica were very nice and seemed as though they could become Eddie's friends quickly.

Alex was about Eddie's height, but his hair was almost white, and he hadn't stopped smiling a silly, crooked smile since Eddie met him. Jessica was tall and thin—definitely one of the boys—with her hair pulled back in a ponytail and her sweatshirt stained with dirt and grass. She was nice, but she didn't maintain a goofy

61

grin like Alex. She was more reserved and a bit shy. Kevin, on the other hand, was pushy and combative right away.

From the moment they arrived, Kevin began questioning Jake. "Who's this kid? No one said he could be in the race."

Kevin looked at Eddie as he talked to Jake. He seemed to be the tough guy of the group. He was a bit taller than the other kids and slightly overweight, but he would probably grow into his body and eventually be very athletic. For now, he was showing his dominance of the group, and Eddie decided he should take the chance. He challenged Kevin and revealed himself to everyone, including his new friend Jake, at the same time.

"I'm Eddie, I just moved here yesterday. Then I went to the North Pole and met Santa's elves. Today I'm going to win this race!"

Kevin paused for a minute, seeming quite confused. "North Pole, Santa's elves ... like Santa Claus? And Christmas?" he asked.

Gasps and mumbles of Christmas memories filled the air as the thought of Christmas began to dance through the mind of each of the other kids. Kevin, definitely not a fan of allowing the new kid to receive this much attention, quipped, "You went to the North Pole? Yeah, and Rudolph is hanging out in my backyard!"

"Rudolph, your backyard ... can you prove it?"

Eddie smiled at Kevin, who snapped back at him, "No, stupid! I was making fun of you!"

The smile never left Eddie's face. He was proud of himself. This bully did exactly what Eddie expected, and it set his plan up perfectly.

"Well, that's too bad because I can prove it." Eddie looked at everyone as they all began to move closer—everyone but Kevin, that is, who stopped everything as quickly as it began.

"Whatever—this is stupid. Let's get the race started. Anyone who isn't ready on time will forfeit."

And that's how Eddie ended up in the Frozen Gauntlet, as they called it. They started on the other side of the frozen lake and had to cross the ice. Eddie's adventure from the previous day prepared him for this, as he used his "run at full speed, jump, and slide across the ice" method. It worked, but not quite as well as the day before. He took a spill and tumbled across the ice, but his momentum kept him moving forward as he ended up on his feet again somewhere between a slide and an attempt at running while passing the center of the lake.

By the time he made it to the opposite side, he was already well ahead of the rest of the group. Next up: climbing the hill, riding his sled down the other side, and the final run through Snowball Alley. More neighborhood kids would be waiting there with endless snowball ammunition, ready to attack.

Because of his initial ice-slide maneuver, Eddie would have won easily if a snowball hadn't hit him from behind when he was making his way up the hill. It hit him right on the back of his head and caused him to fall forward and slip part of the way back down the hill. Kevin was laughing as he caught up with Eddie, who had just regained his footing. Eddie couldn't get mad or get even. The only choice was to act as though it wasn't a big deal. Eddie had a goal, and he had to focus on that goal! He laughed and batted some loose powder toward Kevin and then toward the others behind him. Kevin scowled at Eddie, but the others didn't notice. Instead, they just laughed, threw some loose snow at each other, and continued the race.

The rest of the race was neck and neck for Eddie and Kevin, with the rest of the crew not far behind. They finished the hill climb and made it to their sleds. Then each of them flew down the hill and made it to

Snowball Alley.

During the final leg of the race, they were all running and dodging to the best of their ability, with Eddie slowly pulling away. A loud shriek caused Eddie to look back just in time to see Kevin get hit by a snowball, tumble off of the path, and disappear into the bushes and trees. Eddie attempted to keep running—victory was within sight—but he couldn't finish that way.

Eddie made his way back and shuffled off the path to where Kevin had fallen. "Are you okay?" Eddie asked as he reached a hand to help lift Kevin from the brush he was tangled up in.

Kevin scowled at Eddie, "I'm fine, and I don't need your help!"

Kevin climbed back onto the trail and was on the move again, with Eddie right behind him. The others had all caught up to them and had witnessed Eddie's kind gesture. That was the last thing on anyone's mind, however, for there was less than 100 feet to the finish line and anyone could win! Alex was out in front with Kevin right behind, and Eddie was just passing Jessica and Jake. As they reached the finish line, Eddie had caught up with Kevin, but both were a couple of feet behind Alex, who let out a victorious howl as he won the race.

"You had it, Eddie! Why didn't you finish the race and then come back to help?"

Alex was still smiling from ear to ear, gloating from his victory regardless of how flawed it may have been.

Eddie just shrugged.

"I don't know. He could have been hurt. That seemed more important."

His comment was followed by a moment of silence, as no one really knew how to respond. Finally Kevin, his face red in embarrassment, broke the silence. "I was fine. I don't need help!" Everyone laughed at Kevin's attempt to show how tough he could be.

"What about Christmas, Eddie? And the North Pole?"

Jessica had not forgotten Eddie's promise. He had been to the North Pole, and he said he could prove it.

IX

CHRISTMAS TREES AND
CHRISTMAS CHEER

It was his second day in Brookville, and Eddie had already made friends with a group of kids, along with an Elf Ranger. There was also Kevin. Eddie thought Kevin was just a standard bully from the start, but he now knew it was a bit more complicated. Alex seemed to be closest to Kevin. He was nice in a way that felt as though he was making up for the rough attitude that Kevin brought to the group. After the race, he told Eddie that Kevin would warm up. He just didn't like new people. More than anything, Kevin was a tough kid out of necessity.

Kevin's father hadn't been around since he was five, and his two older brothers were pretty big bullies themselves. Alex revealed that they told Kevin time and time again that they didn't even like him and had tried to convince him to run away about a year ago. After hearing this, Eddie decided that he should give Kevin a break. His brothers sounded evil, and Kevin probably needed another friend more than another enemy right now.

Eddie thought about all of his friends as he walked home, but mostly about how excited they all were for Christmas. Kevin was hesitant and continued to question everything, rolling his eyes and mocking anything Eddie said. It didn't matter, though—Eddie's backpack was now empty. All the extra Christmas decorations he could find at home were with his friends now. They would all be taking Christmas home to their families. Despite everything, Kevin accepted a Christmas movie along with some decorations. Maybe, just maybe, Kevin might warm up to him quickly enough to be part of the plan.

Eddie couldn't contain his excitement. As he passed the lake, he began to run. His legs were moving as fast as he could make them go, but it wasn't fast enough. His parents promised that they would put Christmas lights on the house today, and then they would pick out a Christmas tree and put it up in the evening. Not only had Eddie spread the word of Christmas to his new friends, but his house was set to be the first Christmas display in town. The lights and the tree that would soon be displayed in the front window would be like a public announcement to everyone, proudly and perfectly saying, "Christmas is here!" The smile on Eddie's face grew with this thought as he continued to run up the hill toward home.

When Eddie arrived home, his father pointed to their roof and discussed a game plan with Eddie. They always planned how the lights would be displayed before they started decorating the house.

Each year was always different, mostly because they moved so often. That was the only part that Eddie didn't like. All their moves had caused him to leave so many friends behind. He loved that his father worked as a developer for toys and children's products because he was always allowed to test new toys that had not yet been released. Every so often, Eddie would hear his parents discussing changing markets and contract opportunities with different companies that would soon result in another move to another city. Brookville seemed different. It was a much smaller town than Eddie was used to. While he wasn't sure what opportunity his father had here, he already knew he liked it here. His new friends, Ted, his trip to the North

Pole, the danger of the Shadow Shifters—all of it was like nothing he had ever experienced, and while it was certainly not perfect, Eddie was already connected to Brookville.

As he stretched out the lights and fed them up the ladder to his father, who was hanging them from the front of the house based on the plan they had discussed, Eddie couldn't keep the thought of the Shadow Shifters out of his mind. Tomorrow was Christmas Eve, and he knew that was when they would make their move. Ted and the Elf Rangers would be here, and Eddie would do his part to help. First, he would have to help his dad complete their decorations, though. His focus quickly returned to the task at hand as his dad let out his best impression of Santa, with a "Ho ho ho, and what would you like for Christmas, young man?" Eddie grinned and answered a bit shyly, "It's a secret."

Looking down at Eddie, his dad stopped hanging the lights for a moment. "Well, how do you expect me to tell Santa what you want if I don't know?" Eddie assured him that he had a way to get his letter to Santa. His father nodded with a slight smile and continued to hang the lights, asking Eddie if he wanted to drive to the next town for a tree or go into the forest deep in the back of their property and cut their own tree. That was an easy question for Eddie to answer.

It took a couple of hours to finish hanging the lights. Eddie and his parents would light the house for the first time that evening; he hoped that all of his friends would be watching for it as well. Eddie was thinking of this as he and his father made their way through the forest toward the back of their property. The sunlight didn't penetrate the trees as well as Eddie hoped, and he began thinking of the Shadow Shifters again—this time for good reason, as the sun would set soon. They still needed to choose a tree, cut it, and drag it back on the sled that Eddie was pulling behind him.

In another realm, the creature of the darkness was still watching Eddie. The more he saw, the more the anger within the Shadow continued to grow. He had been staring into the red-hot coals as Brookville transformed and the spirit of Christmas spread. His eyes were no longer endless dark pits but instead glowed red like the coals in front of him, which revealed the maddening silent film that the Shadow could do nothing about—for now.

"Are you sure you don't want to look just a little bit longer?" Alan questioned Eddie after a very quick Christmas tree decision. "Just to be sure we have the right one?" Eddie shook his head. He was sure that this tree was great. He was also sure that if they spent much more time, they risked being out at dark. "Let's get this one and take it home so we can start decorating. We need to get everything up by the time it gets dark!"

It took a bit of time, and Eddie was rushing his dad in a way he never had before, but he had good reason. They were at the door just after the sun met the horizon. Only half of a glowing golden circle remained, casting a beautiful glow across the snow-covered hills and valleys of Brookville. Eddie stopped for a moment to admire the beauty of the light cast by the sun, perhaps appreciating it fully for the first time in his life.

It took quite some time to get the Christmas tree into the house and on the tree stand. By now, every light in the house was on, thanks to Eddie, and the bright light didn't allow anything about their Christmas tree to be hidden. Luckily, it was a fantastic tree. They began moving forward with their annual tradition. It didn't matter where they lived—the tradition could not be broken. They just needed to be together. Eddie's mother had been baking Christmas cookies while Eddie and his dad had decorated the house and picked out a tree.

Now all three of them enjoyed the fresh cookies and

hot cocoa and listened to classic Christmas songs while they decorated their perfect tree, preparing it to be lit and admired. Eddie knew that anyone who happened to be looking in their direction would take notice of the incredible tree that now filled the front window of their home. From where Eddie was standing, the window framed the town square of Brookville—a town square that was still badly in need of decorations and Christmas cheer.

It had been a long day, but the time had finally arrived! Just minutes from now, Eddie and his parents would be standing in the fresh snow, enjoying the colorful glow of Christmas decorations on their new home for the first time.

As Alan flipped the switch, the lights from the Christmas tree lit up the room and illuminated Eddie's face. He smiled. For this moment, the existence of the Shadow Shifters was removed from his mind, and he was just happy. Christmas cheer spread across the room as both of his parents took in the smile on Eddie's face. If only for a few minutes, their concern washed away as well. Moving to Brookville was a great risk. Alan had no contract for work in such a small town with no major corporations. He only had a dream of starting his own business. After endless discussion and months of searching, they finally located the perfect, inspiring little town of Brookville and took a leap of faith.

Finally, Eddie's mother asked, "What do you think, Eddie?"

Eddie looked at his parents. Only one word was needed: "Perfect!" Eddie grinned.

His father chuckled and agreed. "Let's head out front and light the entire house then!"

They all rushed toward the front door and began pulling on their coats and boots. This worry-free moment, however long it would last, was needed by the entire family. As they made their way out the door, Eddie's mother mentioned her surprise that no one else in the entire town seemed to have any decorations.

The carefree moment was over. At least, it was over for Eddie. The thought of the Shadow Shifters was overwhelming—they were halfway out the door and likely tiptoeing on the edge of danger right now. "Wait! Don't go outside yet!!!" Eddie yelled at the top of his lungs as he rushed back inside and up the stairs at full speed.

Unaware of the danger that lurked just outside their well-lit home, his parents chuckled and stepped back into the entryway, looking up the stairs to see what Eddie was so excited about.

After a couple of minutes and some random sounds echoing down the stairs, a colorful glow began to fill the stairwell. Eddie's parents watched as Eddie emerged, fully illuminated. For the first time, they were seeing Eddie as a mobile Christmas decoration in the suit he had crafted. His mother laughed and clapped as he made his way down the stairs, but his father just stared with a slight smile. Eddie had always been crafty and clever, but Alan was especially impressed and even inspired by this creation.

As Eddie reached the bottom of the stairs, he didn't explain or hesitate at all. "Alright, time to see all the decorations!"

"Aren't we already looking at one?" his mother asked. Everyone laughed and made their way to the street in front of the house. No further conversation was necessary; his parents loved the suit, and Eddie was happy that everyone was perfectly protected within the magical glow.

The family stood on the street in front of their home, preparing to trigger their lights with the remote that Alan had made. The streets were silent, with no signs of cars or people, but that didn't mean they were alone. Not even close. In fact, three others watched them intently as they prepared for this celebration. The first was less than 100 feet away. Jake sat in his window waiting for the lights that Eddie had promised him earlier in the day. Just moment ago, he watched the tree light up in their front window. Since that moment, his excitement had been growing until he could barely stand it. He wanted to rip open his window and tell Eddie to light the house decorations now!

Of course, the Elf Rangers were also watching. Well, Ted was watching. He had a soft spot for Eddie and had been keeping an eye on him since their first encounter. More than once, he had taken the portal to Brookville specifically to check on Eddie in person. As much as Ted wanted to protect him, it was obvious to him that Eddie was planning something and might put himself in danger just to help. Eddie cared and wanted to do the right thing, regardless of the consequences. That's part of what Ted loved about him. Combining this quality with Eddie's love for Christmas is what lured the evil forces that were also monitoring Eddie from afar. The Shadow King watched in complete frustration; although it was dark outside, there was still nothing he could do. Eddie was completely surrounded by powerful Christmas lights. Any Shadow Shifter who attempted to get close to him would be eliminated immediately.

As the countdown began in front of the house, both Ted and the Shadow watched with more and more interest. Eddie stood between his parents, his Christmas light suit providing a colorful glow all around them as the magical moment drew nearer.

"Ten, nine, eight ..."

Ted was excited as well as nervous. Eddie was helping so much by bringing Christmas cheer and giving decorations directly to the people of Brookville. He had spread thoughts of Christmas to several of the kids in only a few hours. Ted knew that this would also make Eddie an even bigger target for the Shadow King, though.

"Seven, six, five ..."

Jake was using his shirt to wipe his window clean. It had fogged over completely as he pressed his face against it, breathing directly on the cold glass. He couldn't miss anything—a blurry, foggy view just wouldn't do.

"Four, three, two ..."

The Shadow King, alone in the Fire Viewing Room, moved far away from the coals. His anger and fear peaked as the countdown neared its end. Just the thought of seeing Christmas lights through the coals was enough to instill fear in what was possibly one of the most dreadful creatures the world had ever seen.

The family looked at each other as they reached the end of the countdown.

"One ... LIGHTS!!"

Alan flipped the switch on his remote, and the entire house lit up. The colors shot into the sky. They bounced off the white snow. The glow blanketed their yard and street and illuminated Jake's face as his breath filled his window with fog again. Ted was smiling; this family may have single-handedly saved Christmas for the entire town.

The Fire Viewing Room was now empty. The Shadow King had left.

Eddie looked behind him just in time to see Jake plug in the lights that Eddie had given him. Jake had hung the lights in his bedroom window and was looking down at Eddie. He waved, and Eddie smiled back. Alan stepped behind his family and put his arms around his wife and son. For the first time, he felt comfortable in their new home.

X

THE LAST DAY

It was Christmas Eve morning and, as always, Eddie had awakened early to the smell of his mother making blueberry pancakes. The glow of his Christmas lights still filled his room as sunlight spilled in through his curtains. Eddie made his way downstairs and sat down at the table, where juice and a setting had already been put out for him. He quickly noticed that there was no cup of coffee or newspaper where his dad would normally be sitting. "Where's Dad?" he asked.

His mom smiled and shook her head. "Inspiration apparently struck him last night. He's been in his workshop all night long. I'm sure he'll be in shortly to fill his stomach before getting some sleep."

Eddie scrunched his face, "Wonder what he's working on."

Sophie just shrugged her shoulders as she placed fresh pancakes on Eddie's plate directly from the pan. "Don't worry—we'll know soon enough!" she said as she kissed him on the head and went to let Alan know that breakfast was ready.

Eddie had finished breakfast and was in the garage looking through boxes of more Christmas decorations when his friends arrived. Jake walked into his garage a couple of minutes before Alex and Jessica. Kevin was the only one who hadn't showed up.

The Christmas lights!

Everyone was excited, endlessly raving about how great the lights looked last night. Eddie had not let them down with his promise of an amazing display. They were all excited for Christmas and wanted the entire town to look like Eddie's house. One thing they were not prepared for, however, was the story that Eddie was about to tell.

He started with his trip to the North Pole and meeting Theodore, the Elf Ranger. This all sounded great, but the story soon took a turn as the Shadow Shifters were introduced. To Eddie's surprise, no one was skeptical of him. He had not given them a reason not to trust him yet, plus everyone liked him as soon as they'd met him. Eddie told them that he needed their help, called them all close, and spoke in a tiny whisper.

Eddie was smart, Ted thought. He was watching from the North Pole and couldn't hear what Eddie was saying or read his lips since his friends who huddled close were blocking his face from sight. This meant that no one else could, either, and that's just how Eddie wanted it.

Minutes later, Eddie's friends were leaving, all of them dragging sleds that were loaded down with boxes. Eddie told each of them to be safe, and away they went. Christmas Eve would be a dangerous night for anyone who was spreading Christmas cheer in Brookville this year.

Not more than a minute after Eddie walked back into the house to warm up, his father came in from his workshop and told Eddie that he needed his help. As much as Eddie wanted to stay inside to get warm, he wanted to go out to the workshop more and see what his dad was up to. As they made their way out, Eddie asked his dad what he had been working on. The response was not what Eddie had hoped for. "Be patient. You'll see in just a minute."

What Eddie saw as they entered the workshop wasn't quite what he expected. There were product sketches of stylized winter jackets with notes and details about the features. Next, Eddie spotted his old jacket, but it had been altered. Had his dad been working on clothes instead of toys? Alan quickly explained that he had an idea based on the suit made of Christmas lights that Eddie had made. He showed Eddie his sketches for a line of winter jackets for kids, each sketch showing a different design with glow-in-the-dark panels. "Dad, does my jacket glow in the dark?!" Eddie was excited about the possibility.

"Why don't you put it on and test it for me?" Alan's response wasn't exactly an answer, but Eddie knew exactly what it meant. He did have a glow-in-the-dark jacket now, and he would be a product tester for the pitch book. This never bothered Eddie, but this time he was excited. This was actually his jacket that was being made into a custom product! After he put it on, Alan adjusted the lights in the garage so he could take some photos for his pitch. He would need some light to capture a proper image, but it had to be dark enough to allow the glow-in-the-dark panels to be displayed. A couple of adjustments to the dimming switch, and he had the lighting just right. Eddie's jacket came to life in the dark. He looked down at the glowing patterns that ran down each sleeve and then at the one that covered the chest of the jacket.

"Wow, Dad—this is awesome!"

Alan chuckled as he took some photographs of the jacket that he would later insert into his presentation. After taking several photos, he raised the lights and asked Eddie, "So what do you think?"

Eddie smiled back. "It's great, Dad. Can I wear it?"

Alan told Eddie that of course he could take it. Alan had what he needed to present the concept. Now he would have to build a pitch book and call an old friend on Christmas Eve.

Eddie had been in his room for several hours when his mom called up that dinner would be ready soon. Eddie was putting the finishing touches on his new Christmas light suit. The top half was now attached to his glow-in-the-dark jacket. A quick test proved that it was working just fine. Eddie stopped and looked at his supplies: Christmas light suit, flashlight, his coveted multipurpose Swiss Army Knife, walkie talkie, binoculars, and rope. He wasn't sure what the rope was for but grabbed it just in case. The guys in the movies always ended up using a rope, so he would bring it. He packed everything into his backpack, tucked it away in his closet, and ran downstairs for dinner.

They always had a great Christmas Eve dinner, even

though a giant Christmas dinner would happen the following night. As Eddie reached the bottom of the stairs, the scent of homemade pasta and desserts filled his nose. His mother often cooked Italian, which she had learned from her grandmother, who was the first generation of her family to come to America from northern Italy. She often made homemade noodles, sauce, breads, desserts, and more.

Before sitting down for dinner, Eddie confirmed that the Christmas tree was lit. He walked to the window and saw the outdoor lights filling the yard all the way to the street with multicolored brilliance. The lights in Jake's window were shining brightly as well. This made Eddie happy; Jake had been great so far, and it felt as though they would become best friends.

As Eddie and his parents sat down at the dinner table and began to eat, Alan announced that he had spoken to his old friend Chuck earlier in the day. Chuck had recently become a partner in a company that manufactured and distributed both children's clothing and toys. He seemed impressed with the concept and presentation that Alan had assembled. The concept and initial sketches were fresh and fun. Chuck would meet with his partners in the new year and set up a meeting with Alan if they were interested in learning more. Alan smiled as his family cheered and celebrated this step toward success.

"Your mom said that several friends came to see you today. You gave away some Christmas decorations, is that right?"

Eddie was unsure if his Dad was upset that he gave away decorations. It was important, though—he had to do it to protect everyone and to protect Christmas itself. Eddie couldn't tell them that, though, since they wouldn't believe him, and he couldn't lead his parents to the North Pole portal. He had promised Ted that he wouldn't show anyone.

"Yes, I gave my new friends leftover decorations."

Eddie answered simply and honestly. It was his only choice. Alan nodded his head.

"Good job! I haven't noticed decorations on a single home or business. Hopefully you've turned that around and we'll start seeing some real Christmas cheer in this town!"

After dinner, Eddie was helping his parents clean up when he heard a thud upstairs. Neither of his parents noticed, but it definitely happened, and it sounded as if it came from his bedroom. As he slowly crept up the steps, he heard another sound. It was definitely in his bedroom. He could see the glow of his Christmas lights, so it couldn't be a Shadow Shifter; if he'd learned anything about them from his trip to the North Pole, he knew they couldn't survive within the glow of Christmas lights.

Eddie grew more afraid with each step that took him closer to uncertainty. Did the Shadow Shifters send someone else—or some*thing* else—after him? It was Christmas Eve, and they were running out of time. They could be desperate. Eddie could hear his own breathing as he approached his partially open bedroom door. Sudden movement caused Eddie to freeze, but it was too late to run. Someone appeared in the doorway and pulled him into the room with one swift movement. For a moment Eddie knew he had been captured, but Ted's face quickly came into focus.

Ted calmed him. "Shhh, it's just me!"

Eddie breathed a sigh of relief.

"What are you doing here? Shouldn't you be working with the other Elf Rangers to stop the Shadow Shifters? Tonight is Christmas Eve!"

Ted assured him that they were prepared and that they would save Christmas. "We need you to stay at home and stay safe, Eddie. I don't want to be concerned for your safety tonight."

Eddie nodded in agreement. He actually didn't

agree, but he didn't want to slow down the efforts of the Elf Rangers. He had a feeling that they would need his help. They would need all the help they could get. Ted told him to enjoy his first Christmas in Brookville. Then, with a couple of quick moves, he bounced out the window and down the corner of the house. Eddie watched him disappear into the darkness. The sun had almost fully set, and night was now upon them.

XI

THE SHADOW SHIFTERS ARE COMING

It had been more than an hour since Eddie's parents had gone to bed. Eddie had been lying in his bed quietly, waiting for the right time. That time was now. As he made his way downstairs, Eddie thought that this was not the best night to learn that every stair in his new home creaked—loudly.

"Leave the town of Brookville and let these people enjoy their lives. Go back to your lair and don't return. Do that and none of you will be harmed."

Ted communicated this warning to the Shadow King who, for the moment, stood on the opposite side of the pond. He was all alone against an army of Elf Rangers. The deep, ominous voice that replied was quick and full of hate.

"I own Brookville now, and there's nothing you can

do about it! Now, run away, Ted, and take your little elves before you regret your decision to come here and face me."

With that, he disappeared from sight.

All forty fully trained Elf Rangers were here to protect the people of Brookville, and they were all on high alert now, color wands and spotlights in hand, night vision on. Most of this army had seen action against evil forces before, including the Shadow Shifters.

They were ready for action. At least they thought they were. From nowhere, a group of Shadow Shifters appeared and surrounded five Elf Rangers. Four disappeared too quickly for anyone to respond, taking the Elves with them, while one was bathed in a multicolored flash of light emitted by Ted's color wand. The large creature of darkness soaked up the light like an old sponge. In the blink of an eye, light rays began rushing back out from the darkness, a high-pitched shriek filled the air, and light exploded from the darkness.

The Shifter was gone. Ted rushed over to his fellow Ranger, who now lay on the ground. His eyes were dark, and he was unresponsive.

The remaining Rangers surrounded them with their wands in hand, ready for another attack.

"Come on, Rachel—come back to us."

As Ted talked to his fellow Ranger, she began to move a bit, and her eyes were shifting back from black to their normal light green. She would return from the darkness soon, but Ted would have to focus on the Shadow Shifters and Brookville. He left her in the care of two other Rangers. The Shadow Shifters' tactics had changed. They would not let themselves be seen unless they were going to attack. This was clever and definitely posed a problem for Ted. The Elf Rangers would have to be quicker and more alert than ever. Ted had already lost four Rangers, and another was recovering now.

"Alright team, be alert!" Ted yelled to his troops as the clock in the town hall began ringing eleven o'clock. Christmas was one hour away. They had to make their stand.

"We have to let our wands and spotlights recharge between flashes. Don't be tricked into using them when it's not necessary. We don't want to be unprotected against the Shifters. These nasty Shifters have learned to stay hidden until they are ready to attack. We won't have much time to react!"

With that, there was another attack. This time, the Shifters came in waves. Flashes of color filled the air on the edge of the lake, while spots of darkness appeared around the troop of Elf Rangers. One Ranger after another was enveloped in darkness while an occasional shriek and burst of light meant the end of another Shadow Shifter. The battle was in full swing, and before Ted knew it he was down to just an army of ten.

Thirty captured Elf Rangers were now gathered in the town square. They were unresponsive, currently stuck in darkness and awaiting whatever fate the Shadow King might have planned for them. Ted had never been in this situation before. He had to reach them and bring them back before anything worse happened—before they were lost for good.

"Stick to the plan. Protect yourselves and protect Brookville!" Ted shouted to the remaining soldiers.

They all barked in unison, "Yes, sir!"

Ted rushed ahead on his own without another word and disappeared over the hill. He had his color wand in hand as he entered the town square.

In the middle of everything, in the exact place where Eddie imagined decorations upon his first visit, were all of Ted's soldiers. They were on the ground, and none of them were moving. Shadow Shifters were swarming around them, keeping the Rangers' minds lost in darkness and seemingly preparing for something big.

Ted slowed his approach, as he didn't want any of the Shifters to notice him before he was ready to attack. Ted heard a sound behind him and froze. Not by choice, though—he was frozen by the Shadow King himself.

"You are the only Elf Ranger that I would risk myself for, Ted."

The words slipped off the tongue of the Shadow King like a snake. Ted's eyes were black, and his body was like a statue as he stood frozen.

Ted could see nothing but black. Complete darkness. He felt fear for the first time in his recent memory. He could hear the Shadow King whispering sinister words to him and could feel his icy touch as he continued to push Ted's mind further into darkness. Memories began to fade, his thoughts began to slip into nothingness, and his fear grew stronger. *I failed*. This was the last conscious thought that made its way into Ted's mind before it became frozen, locked on evil and darkness.

XII

LIGHT FROM DARKNESS

Less than a hundred feet from this scene, Eddie and Jake watched in silence. They were hiding nearby, protected by the shadows of Jake's mother's coffee shop. Watching these evil Shifters take his friend made Eddie's fear transform into anger.

He had to do something.

Eddie whispered, "Jake, you stay here. You have to stay out of sight until I lure everyone into the town square."

Jake looked at Eddie and nodded. He was afraid. Although Eddie had told him about the Shadow Shifters and the Elf Rangers and that the battle for Christmas was certain to happen, he couldn't imagine how dangerous and scary it might be, until now.

Eddie ran as fast as he could. He ran directly toward

the Rangers who were now stuck in the darkness. He ran directly toward the group of Shadow Shifters. He ran directly toward danger, and he didn't care. He was within 20 feet of the Shifters as he emerged from the shadows of the coffee shop and gained their attention. Just as he reached for the switch on his suit, one powerful Shifter appeared right next to him. Eddie's finger touched the switch that would activate the lights and eliminate the Shadow Shifters just as Vesh made contact with him.

Eddie's mind immediately went dark as Vesh let out an eerie and celebratory evil hiss. The Shadow King would be happy that Vesh had captured the boy who brought Christmas back to Brookville.

As he heard the hiss, Eddie focused on the world in front of him with everything he had: the disabled Elf Rangers, his friend Ted, and his home—Brookville. Eddie's mind was strong enough to escape the darkness for a moment, and that's all it took to create colorful, beautiful light!

All the nearby Shifters vanished behind the explosions of light. The last trace of this group of Shadow Shifters was the shriek that each of them let out once the powerful light struck them. These terrible sounds echoed through the nearby hills as they were carried away by the wind. The glowing pits where Vesh's eyes should have been seemed to peer deep into Eddie's just before the light burst from his body and he released a similar high-pitched shriek and disappeared.

Eddie lay motionless on the ground. Through all the terror, he felt as if he had seen a touch of humanity in the eyes of this Shadow Shifter just before he vanished into nothingness. Eddie continued to lie in the snow, feeling confused by what he thought he saw.

The Shadow Shifters were gone, but the Rangers were still stuck in darkness.

Jake was still. Everything was. Jake looked around for a minute, but there was no sound, no movement, nothing. He knew he had an assignment, but he wanted to help his new friend. Eddie needed him now.

Making his way across the snow-covered ground, Jake was shielded by the glow of Eddie's Christmas light suit. Jake knelt next to his friend and began to talk to him, telling Eddie that they needed him to finish this and that he didn't want to forget Christmas again. Eddie groaned and began moving. His mind was still reeling. After a moment, he realized where he was and became painfully aware of what had happened.

"Jake, you can't be here—you have to signal the team!"

Just as Eddie spoke, darkness fell around them. Something in Eddie's suit had failed. He flipped the switch off and on again. Nothing.

"Hurry—get out of here, Jake. Forget the trap. Start the plan now!"

Wasting no time, Jake nodded and took off running back toward the coffee shop.

"Don't worry …"

Jake stopped there.

He stopped talking, stopped running, stopped breathing.

Eddie was trying to revive Ted but looked up to see a giant wall of Shadow Shifters between Jake and the coffee shop. The remaining Rangers hadn't made it to the town square yet, either. As far as Eddie knew, the Shadow Shifters had captured them as well.

This was it—they had failed, and Christmas would be lost.

Eddie didn't know what to do, but the thought of his mind being stuck in darkness again caused his heart to skip a beat and his stomach to turn. What could he do? There had to be something.

The Shadow Shifters taunted them, hissing and growling before the Shadow King finally came forward.

His voice was deep and powerful. As he spoke, Eddie could both feel and hear his voice.

"You can stop searching for a solution Eddie ... because there isn't one."

The Shadow King paused as he touched Jake, who was rendered unconscious immediately. Eddie watched as Jake fell to the ground.

Eddie felt responsible for all of this. He should have been able to win. Now his friend was lost, and Christmas would be lost forever, too. But that wasn't even the worst part of the Shadow King's plan. As Eddie was about to learn, this was going to get much worse.

"I've won," the Shadow King said. "The Elf Rangers and Santa Claus can do nothing to save you once we turn your mind to darkness. Once there is no Christmas spirit left in this town, they will be powerless. I will cast darkness over all of Brookville. All your friends will become my servants."

The King continued, "Finally, I will be able to travel back and relieve Santa Claus of his Christmas duties as I take control of the North Pole. Say goodbye to Christmas as you know it, Eddie."

The Shadow King began to swell as he slowly approached Eddie, savoring the moment when he would finally take control of Brookville for good and remove this pest of a child who had nearly prevented his glorious victory.

Eddie remained on the ground as tears welled in his eyes. He didn't know what to do. He had failed everyone. The Shadow King hovered over the top of Eddie and placed his face just inches from Eddie's. Glowing pits where the Shadow King's eyes should be stared right into Eddie's eyes as he asked, "Any last words?"

"I've got some last words."
An unknown voice shouted from the dark area near the coffee shop.

"Merry Christmas!"

Suddenly a blast of multicolored lights illuminated all of them as the Shadow King vanished from sight. The remaining Shifters were not so quick; they began bursting into light, one after another, each of them producing the same hideous shriek that signaled the end of their terror just before disappearing for good.

"Are you okay, Eddie?" Kevin shouted as he smiled down at Eddie. Fighting through fear and tears, Eddie smiled back and gave him the thumbs-up sign.

"Light 'em up!" Eddie shouted back.

One after another, the houses and small shops began to light up around the town square. Eddie saw Alex and Jessica, along with a couple of the other kids who had been throwing snowballs during the snow race.

All the Christmas lights Eddie had given to his friends had been put to good use. The entire town square was glowing now, and everyone who had been taken by the Shadow King began to awaken, returning from the darkness to a transformed Brookville filled with beautiful and bright multicolored lights. Then something even more unexpected happened.

Even Eddie was surprised when he heard it. Someone was playing a Christmas song in the now fully illuminated town square. One by one, people began peering out their windows and stepping out onto their front stoops to see what was happening.

Ted began barking orders right away. People were coming, and the Rangers couldn't afford to be seen by everyone. They had to evacuate immediately.

"Back to home base!" he commanded the Rangers. There had already been more than a half dozen witnesses in Eddie's friends. Ted didn't want the entire town to see the Rangers in action. They rushed off into the darkness toward the portal as the town square began to fill up with Brookville's residents. Ted took cover but continued to watch as people gathered, taking in the sights and sounds of Christmas.

Eddie watched and smiled as everyone enjoyed the lights and music. Nearby, Ted focused on him again.

This kid is special, he thought.

Eddie hadn't listened to any of the warnings that Ted gave him and hadn't shown fear in the face of danger. He did what he thought was right for the town he had moved to just days before. Ted was impressed with his bravery and his ability to bring people together.

His moment of admiration for Eddie was cut short as he realized that the clock would strike midnight soon and it would be Christmas Day. There was still a ton of work to do before morning!

All of Eddie's friends from the race had joined him now, including Kevin, who had become an unexpected hero. Jake walked over with his head down. He was clearly embarrassed that he hadn't followed through with his task and had abandoned his post to come to help Eddie. This move nearly ended the entire plan, as the coffee shop was the signal to their friends to light up the town. Jessica, Alex, and the other kids who had helped place Christmas lights throughout the town square were there as well. Everyone was looking to Eddie, waiting for him to laugh, to celebrate, to say anything.

It didn't take long.

"That was brave of you to run out and try to save me. Thank you, Jake—you're a good friend."

All the kids cheered for Jake, gave him high fives, and patted him on the back. Eddie looked at him with admiration. When he had run out to save the Rangers, he had his light suit for protection. It may have been risky, but he had a plan. Jake, on the other hand, didn't have a light suit—only a desire to help his friend.

Jake just smiled and shrugged. Then he looked at Eddie and said, "Ahh, you woulda done the same for me."

Eddie put his arm around Jake's shoulder and smiled.

The teenagers and adults paid no attention to the group of kids who were talking and cheering. Instead, they continued laughing and talking loudly among themselves about how beautiful everything looked. They were completely unaware of who had hung the lights throughout the town, and no one even thought to ask. Meanwhile, following congratulations from all of his friends, Eddie said he wanted to tell them one more thing.

"You were all awesome, but this wouldn't have happened without Kevin. He didn't have to risk himself, but he came out of nowhere and saved the day when I thought we had lost."

Kevin was standing toward the back of the crowd. His face turned red as everyone turned toward him. He mumbled a bit, trying to find the right words to say, but he was stumped.

After a few moments, the kids interrupted his failed attempts to say something meaningful with celebratory cheers. They all jumped on top of him, forming a dogpile like a winning baseball team. No one needed to say anything more—Christmas had been saved, and that was enough.

XIII

CHRISTMAS MORNING

The edges of the windowpanes were covered in snow that had fallen throughout the night. Eddie, still groggy from sleep, looked at the snow and the lights. He had gone to sleep much later than normal last night.

Also, sneaking back into the house hadn't worked as well as sneaking out had. Eddie's parents were waiting when he returned, and punishment would be coming. Or so Eddie thought. But it never happened.

His parents were upset that he had left the house without permission, especially after dark. He couldn't tell them the reason he had to go, but they already knew why he left. At least, they had a reason that Eddie quickly agreed with.

His parents explained that the lights and music

looked great from their house and that it woke them up as well. They told Eddie that he should have awakened them for the Christmas celebration rather than walking down to see it himself. Eddie nodded and said no more.

They proceeded to usher him upstairs to bed, and although his mind was filled with all the events of the night, he couldn't fight his fatigue anymore. He was exhausted and fell asleep right away.

The next morning, Eddie lay in bed as the light filled his room, thinking about everything that had happened and smiling. His plan came together in an unexpected way with unexpected heroes, but the important thing was that it worked. Christmas was safe, and the Shadow Shifters were gone.

Eddie climbed out of bed and pulled some socks on his feet to protect them from the cold wood floor, walked to his window, and looked out at his new hometown.

Christmas lights were still shining in the town square, and fresh snow that was mostly untouched blanketed the town. It was perfect.

Eddie always felt that fresh snow was a sign of a great Christmas Day ahead. Before leaving the window, he picked up his binoculars from the side table and scanned the lake and the portal to the North Pole. He saw nothing, put down the binoculars, and turned to leave the room.

Since morning had come and it was light outside, he reached down to unplug the Christmas lights in his room. Instead, he took a look back at them, thought of his new friend Ted, and decided to leave them glowing as he walked downstairs.

As expected, his parents were sitting in the living room on the couch near the tree, drinking coffee and reading. They were patiently waiting for Eddie to come downstairs so that Christmas morning and gift opening could begin.

"Merry Christmas!" Eddie shouted.

His mother jumped, obviously startled, while his father looked up and laughed. Eddie rushed down and hugged them both and then hopped onto the empty spot on the couch next to them. It only took a moment for his parents to begin with presents and Christmas morning festivities.

His mother jumped up and headed toward the kitchen. "I'm going to bring some juice for everyone. Would you like hot cocoa too, Eddie?" she asked as she shuffled through cabinets.

"Yes, please!" Eddie shouted as his father began to look through the gifts that were under the tree. Turning back to Eddie, he shook one of them just a bit.

"Looks like you've got a big gift over here, bud."

Eddie wondered what it could be. He hadn't asked for any toys this year. He definitely didn't ask for anything from Santa that would come in a box that big.

"Is that from you and Mom?" Eddie asked.

Alan immediately shook his head with a smile.

"Santa," he responded.

Eddie was puzzled. There was only one thing in his Christmas letter to Santa, and it wouldn't come in a box. They always saved the biggest gifts for last. Eddie knew this mystery gift would be the last one to be opened today. The wait was going to be impossible.

The gifts started as they always did. Socks, underwear, shirts, and sweaters led the way for Eddie. His parents opened their clothes as well. Eddie was ready to move forward. Next came some action figures and a build-your-own electronics kit that both surprised and excited Eddie. The days of having to repurpose electronics he found around the house had come to an end. Now he had supplies of his own, and maybe, just maybe, his parents' remote controls would be safe.

Though there were still gifts with his name on them, Eddie stopped his parents and dug out their gifts from him.

"They're both for both of you. Open them together!"

Eddie's parents looked at each other and then at Eddie as they began opening the gifts at the same time. As the wrapping paper revealed each gift, Eddie watched the smiles overtake his parents' faces.

Each gift had been custom made by Eddie. His mother opened a framed photograph of the three of them that Eddie had taken as they were all unpacking their new home just days before. In the last couple of days, Eddie had printed, framed, and customized this on his own to include the word *Home* on the frame.

The second gift, which his father unwrapped, was a larger box by design but a much smaller gift. This gift was a handwritten gift certificate promising a full evening of undisturbed Mom and Dad time when Eddie would both behave himself and take care of himself.

Alan and Sophie couldn't keep from laughing and hugging their son tightly.

After each of them opened a few more gifts, only one remained. It was the large box—large enough that Eddie himself could fit comfortably inside it.

As he began to peel the wrapping paper, Eddie noticed that the box tipped slightly. He paused for a moment and then pushed the box. It rocked back slightly. Eddie stopped tearing paper and knelt in front of the box while placing his fingers near the bottom edge.

They slipped right underneath. There was no bottom to this box.

As he began to lift it, a wheel with spokes was revealed, then pedals, a chain, and a brightly colored frame. It was the bicycle that Eddie had noticed in the display at the toy store!

Eddie couldn't believe it—he really wanted this bicycle, but he didn't even ask for it. Why had Santa brought it to him? And how did he even know!? Eddie climbed onto the bicycle as he remembered seeing it for the first time in the display window at the toy store, hanging in midair with a crocodile waiting below.

__The ground was covered with snow now, but with spring would also come bicycle stunts__, Eddie thought.

A soft thud followed by two more quickly captured Eddie's attention. The sounds were coming from upstairs. His attention immediately shifted from the bike to the sounds. His parents didn't seem to notice them, and Eddie began to think that perhaps only he could hear the Christmas elves.

He wanted to run upstairs, but he couldn't run away from his largest and coolest gift. He would have to have a good reason to go up to his room at that moment without causing his parents to become suspicious.

Ring, ring. Ring, ring.

Eddie was saved by the telephone. It never rang on Christmas Day. This must be important or else a wrong number. Either one would give him a chance to run up to his room, which he did right away.

There was no one in his room, but as he went over toward the window, he noticed something new. Sitting on his side table was a snow globe with an envelope underneath. Eddie picked up the globe and looked at it. It was the North Pole. As he shook it, he heard the faint sound of bells. He watched the snow fall inside the snow globe world and felt a magical warmth wash over his body. The envelope had "Eddie" written across the front in gold letters.

Shuffling through some random items, Eddie quickly found his binoculars. He grabbed them and looked toward the portal, where he saw Ted for the first time today. Just as he did, Ted opened the portal and disappeared inside.

Eddie felt a sense of sadness come over him. He wanted to see Ted again and talk to him. He continued to look through his binoculars, hoping to see something special. It didn't take long for a head to pop out of the portal. Ted looked right at him, smiled, and waved. Eddie smiled and waved back before Ted disappeared and the hatch closed.

Eddie put down the binoculars and looked at the snow globe. Would he ever see Ted again? He looked at the letter that was left behind.

Upon opening the letter, he realized that this was not a letter from Ted. The letter was from Santa, and it was written directly to Eddie!

Eddie had received a letter back from Santa for the first time ever! He began to read excitedly.

Dear Eddie,

You were extremely brave in helping my Elf Rangers battle the Shadow Shifters and even more helpful in spreading the word about Christmas throughout the town of Brookville. For both of these things, I thank you.

However, I am even more impressed by the letter you sent me this year. When you first saw the bicycle in the toy store, your eyes lit up, but you didn't ask for it. You did deserve this gift, though, so I hope you enjoy and appreciate it.

With everything that was happening around you, I was proud to see you ask for a gift that is much more thoughtful and important. Rather than ask for any of the toys that you've seen this year, you asked to be able to stay in Brookville, a town that you barely know. You asked for friends that you will not have to leave again. For such a thoughtful, brave, and amazing boy, I think I can help with that.

Merry Christmas, Eddie!
SC

P.S. Ted will be in touch to give you a personal briefing on the Shadow Shifters. We'll need eyes in Brookville to notify us when they decide to return, and I can't think of a better young man to entrust with the fate of Christmas.

I also remember overhearing a curious boy who hoped to tour the Toy Factory after sneaking into the North Pole. It's about time I grant that wish, too.

Pure joy. That's what Eddie felt after reading the letter. Santa Claus had personally thanked him and responded to his Christmas wish. He would see Ted again, he would help the Elf Rangers again, and he would see the Toy Factory at the North Pole!

Best Christmas ever!

As Eddie sat on the edge of his bed, smiling and looking at the letter from Santa, the ink began to fade. Within seconds, the words were gone and he was holding a blank page.

"What now?" Eddie asked aloud to no one.

With that, Eddie heard the faint sound of bells again, followed by the sound of shoes slapping the wooden staircase rapidly. His father burst through the door.

"We did it, Eddie. Your suit—the glow-in-the-dark jacket! I have a contract to begin working on it!"

Alan picked Eddie up and spun him in a circle. They both laughed and cheered as Sophie stepped into the doorway and watched.

"They're getting a contract underway on Christmas Day?" she asked.

Alan set Eddie back down next to the bed and turned to her.

"Yes, apparently the owner of the new company that Chuck has partnered with said that Christmas Day is a very busy work day for him. Chuck apologized for interrupting but said that they want to get started right away and thought that the news might be a welcome Christmas gift."

"So we get to stay here so you can make it?" Eddie looked up at both of his parents.

Alan turned and knelt in front of Eddie.

"Do you want to stay here, Eddie?"

Eddie looked up to his Dad and nodded his head.

"Well, good, because with this new product line, it looks like we'll be able to set up production in Brookville and stay here for a long time!"

Eddie smiled and turned back toward the window. He looked toward the lake and then picked up his snow globe. The company was owned by Santa Claus. Eddie knew it.

"Hey, where'd you get that snow globe, Eddie?" his mom asked as she stepped closer and pushed his hair back from his forehead.

"One of my new friends gave it to me."

His mom smiled back and said it was a nice gift.

"Since we have such a beautiful white Christmas, what do you two think about building an igloo?" Alan looked at both of them as Eddie nodded his head yes.

"Well, let's go!" his dad cheered as he ran down the stairs with Eddie and his mother following closely behind.

They all slipped into boots and coats and mittens and ran out the door. As they were choosing the location and began to outline their igloo construction, Jake stepped onto his front porch and shouted across the street.

"Hey, Eddie, what are you doing?"

Eddie looked up at his friend and shouted back, "We're gonna build an igloo!"

"Cool! Can I help?"

Without hesitation Eddie shouted back, "Yeah, come on over!"

Jake came running across the street, stopping right in front of Eddie. After a moment's pause, Jake broke the silence.

"Merry Christmas, Eddie."
"Merry Christmas to you too, Jake."

They smiled and began gathering snow for their igloo.

Brookville was home.

THE ADVENTURES OF EDDIE CONTINUE...

Next up in the "Adventures of Eddie" series, Eddie and his pals venture off to summer camp, only to discover that they aren't alone. There is something in the woods just outside their cabin, and it's not friendly!

Learn more about what's next by visiting Eddie online at eddiesnextadventure.com.

Turn to page 121 to read an excerpt from the upcoming adventure.

Eddie Versus the Creature in the Woods
A Mission to Save Summer Camp

He heard it again, and it was unmistakable this time. Those were definitely footsteps, followed by a loud sniffing sound. Jake shivered and pulled up his blanket, covering part of his face. He was afraid and didn't know what to do. The rest of the cabin was completely dark and quiet except for the loud, rhythmic snore that was clearly coming from Kevin in the next bunk. Had everyone else fallen asleep already? Jake whispered up toward the top bunk, hoping he had one companion who was still awake.

"Eddie, I think you were right ... there's something out there."

No reply. Jake sat still, holding his breath and listening to the footsteps grow louder as they moved closer to the cabin. He tried once more.

"Eddie ..." he whispered.

Just then, Eddie's face appeared from the top bunk. He was wearing his headlamp, which was on the lowest setting, barely bright enough for them to be able to see each other. Eddie put his finger to his lips and silently mimed "shhhh," then reached up and turn off his headlamp.

Darkness.

They were both lying in silence with only a hint of moonlight coming in through the edge of the partially open window shade near the cabin door. There wasn't enough light to see anything inside the cabin, but they could see the shape of the window and some silhouettes outside, and unfortunately they could still hear the footsteps.

The creature that approached could only be feet away from the cabin now. Both Eddie and Jake were still, with their eyes locked on the only thing they could make out in the darkness—the window.

Suddenly there was motion. Something had passed by the window.

A dark figure.

It was too dark to tell what it was, but Eddie definitely saw it. He whispered to the bottom bunk.

"Jake, did you—"

"Yes!" Jake shot back.

Both of them continued to lie motionless, with only the snore that rumbled from Kevin's nostrils to disrupt the otherwise silent and motionless cabin. Unsure what was to come, Eddie's mind began to race. He had to think of something—some kind of plan.

But there was no time; the cabin door shuddered and the doorknob rattled. The creature Eddie had seen last night had come for them, and there was nothing they could do. Jake pulled his covers over his head, and Eddie braced for the worst. The doorknob began to twist, and the creaky door hinges announced the arrival of their unwelcome visitor. Before either of them could say a word or do anything, the silhouetted creature that now framed the doorway made its move toward them with something in its hand. There was a clicking sound and …

Made in the USA
Middletown, DE
26 November 2018